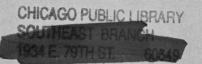

24C

12|10

THE ANGEL'S MISTAKE
STORIES OF CHELM

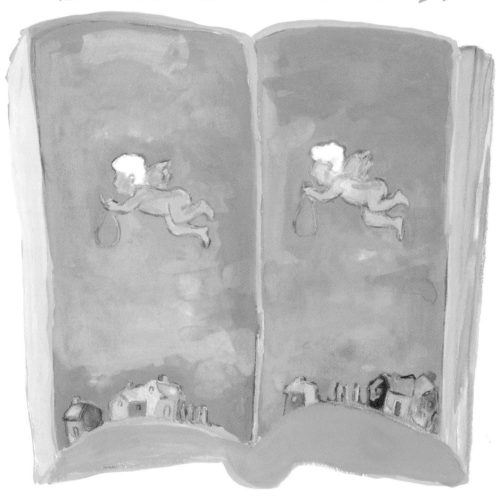

By Francine Prose
Pictures by Mark Podwal

Greenwillow Books, New York

AUTHOR'S NOTE

Chelm is an actual town in Poland, located southeast of Lublin and dating from the Middle Ages. No one knows why its inhabitants have for centuries been the subject of humorous Yiddish folktales about the slow-witted and endearingly silly "wise men and women of Chelm." Equally mysterious is the origin of the traditional legend about an angel spilling a bag of foolish souls over the town.

Additional stories about Chelm can be found in Nathan Ausubel's A *Treasury of Jewish Folklore* (New York: Crown, 1958) and Alan Unterman's *Dictionary of Jewish Lore and Legend* (London: Thames & Hudson, 1991).

Gouache and colored pencils were used for the full-color art.
The text type is Novarese Medium.
Text copyright © 1997 by Francine Prose
Illustrations copyright © 1997 by Mark Podwal
Printed in Singapore by Tien Wah Press
First Edition 10 9 8 7 6 5 4 3 2 1

Library of Congress Cataloging-in-Publication Data

Prose, Francine, (date)
The angel's mistake: stories of Chelm /
retold by Francine Prose ;
pictures by Mark Podwal.
p.   cm.
Includes bibliographical references.
Summary: Explains how a botched mission by two
angels created the town of fools known as Chelm.
ISBN 0-688-14905-7 (trade)
ISBN 0-688-14906-5 (lib. bdg.)
[1. Chelm (Chelm, Poland)—Folklore.
2. Jews—Europe, Eastern—Folklore.
3. Folklore—Europe, Eastern.]
I. Podwal, Mark H., (date) ill.   II. Title.
PZ8.1.P9348An   1997   398.2'089924—dc20
[E]   96-7465   CIP   AC

For Neil, Johanna, and Sarah
—F. P.

For Paul
—M. P.

Long ago, on a lovely day, two angels flew through the sky. Since no angel is ever asked to do two things at once, each angel carried one bag. One of the bags was full of intelligent souls. The other angel carried a bag of souls that were . . . not so clever.

The angels' mission was to sprinkle the towns and cities with souls, making sure that each place got an equal mixture of smart people and fools.

But the angels were so busy enjoying their flight on that lovely day that the angel in charge of the foolish souls swooped too low over a rocky mountain top. . . .

The bag of souls snagged on the jagged peak—and broke!

All the stupid souls spilled out, rolled down the side of the mountain . . .

and landed in one little town.

The town of Chelm.

Of course, the people of Chelm were too stupid to know that they were stupid.

They called themselves the wise men and women of Chelm, the smartest town in the world.

They had an answer for everything.

When the man who woke them for morning prayers got too old to go from house to house, they took their doors off the hinges and brought them to him so he could knock on their doors without leaving his yard.

They went barefoot in the snow so their shoes wouldn't get wet.

When it rained, they wore their hats upside down to keep them dry.

They made jam from the pits of peaches and plums and threw the rest of the fruit away.

Once when the rabbi bought a fish in the market, he took it home in his pocket. When the fish's tail slapped the rabbi's face, the people decided to punish the fish by drowning it in the lake!

The wise men and women of Chelm had many meetings in order to put their brilliant minds together and solve their problems.

They debated what to do with the earth from the hole they had dug for the foundation for a new synagogue. They decided to dig another hole and put the earth in that. But then what should they do with the earth from the second hole?

And when they finally constructed the synagogue, they built it without a roof so their prayers could rise directly to heaven.

Mostly they discussed how to make the town brighter, because it was often dark at the base of their mountain.

The people decided they would get more light if they removed the rock on the mountaintop, the rock on which the bag of souls had snagged.

They climbed the mountain and lifted the boulder and slowly carried it down.

They were almost at the bottom when a passing stranger asked, "Why don't you just roll it?"

So they slowly, slowly carried the rock all the way back up to the mountaintop, and this time they let it roll.

Still the town was in shadow.

"Let's move the mountain!" they said. Everyone ran to the mountain and pushed.

The mountain stayed where it was.

And the town remained dark and gloomy.

The citizens of Chelm agreed that the days weren't so bad—at least the sun shone for a short while before it went behind the mountain. But the nights—especially the moonless nights—were very dark, and they often fell and hurt themselves.

Finally one Chelm wise man happened to glance
into a water barrel.

He saw the moon's reflection in the water
and said, "Look! The moon's in here!

"Let's bring the barrel inside and keep the moon around to shine when we need it!"

But whenever they brought the barrel indoors, the moon vanished.

They had almost stopped trying to light the
night when a child cried, "I know how to make it
bright! Let's build a fire!"

"Yes," agreed the children. "A fire in the middle
of the schoolroom floor where we can keep it going
even when it rains."

"Oh, what smart children we have!" said the people of Chelm.

The children piled some broken desks in the center of the schoolroom floor. The grownups lit the fire. Then everyone went outside and watched the flames through the windows.

The light grew brighter. The fire got hotter.

After a while someone said, "I think the school's burning down."

At last one of the children was sent to call the fire department, which came with its fire engine—a wagon heaped with logs.

"Throw the logs on the flames!" the firemen said. "That's how we'll put out the fire—by smothering it with wood!"

But of course the wood made the fire burn harder. By morning the town of Chelm was a heap of smoking ashes.

"What now?" wailed the citizens of Chelm as they looked at their ruined town.

They tried and tried to rebuild it—but their
plans never came out right.

They scattered everywhere—which was just what
the angels had intended on that lovely day when they
flew over the little town of Chelm.

So the Grand Rabbi of Chelm decided they all should leave the town.

Some went this way, some went that way, some to this city, some to that, a few here, a few there.